CLASS BABY

Miss Colman and Mrs Springer stepped into the room. "Hi, Miss Colman," Mrs Springer replied. "I just brought this in for Natalie." Mrs Springer held up a brown paper bag. "She forgot it this morning. It is her underwear. Her ballet lesson is this afternoon, and Natalie needs a change of clothes." Mrs Springer waved to Natalie. Then she left.

I am dead meat, said Natalie to herself.

Also in the Kids in Miss Colman's Class series:

Look out for:

More school stories from Young Hippo!

Class Four's Wild Week
Malcolm Yorke

Nightingale News
Odette Elliott

Off to School
Jean Chapman

The Grott Street Gang
Terry Deary

Whizz Bang and the Crocodile Room
Susan Gates

Jannie, Bobby, Tammy, Sara
Ian, Leslie, Hank, Terri
Nancy, Omar, Audrey, Chris, Miss Colman
Karen, Hannie, Ricky, Natalie

Scholastic Children's Books,
Commonwealth House, 1–19 New Oxford Street,
London WC1A 1NU, UK
a division of Scholastic Ltd
London – New York – Toronto – Sydney – Auckland

First published in the US by Scholastic Inc., 1996
First published in the UK by Scholastic Ltd, 1997

Copyright © Ann M. Martin, 1996

ISBN 0 590 19088 1

Typeset by Rowland Phototypesetting Ltd,
Bury St Edmunds, Suffolk
Printed by Cox & Wyman Ltd, Reading, Berks.

10 9 8 7 6 5 4 3 2 1

THE KIDS IN MISS COLMAN'S CLASS

4.
CLASS BABY

ANN M. MARTIN

Illustrated by Charles Tang

Hippo

This book is for
Kate Gibbel

NATALIE SPRINGER

Natalie Springer yawned and stretched. She sat up in bed. She peered out of the window. It was still dark outside. As dark as midnight. But Natalie knew it was time to get up. She liked getting up early, when it was still dark. When she felt as if she were the only one in the world who was awake.

Let me see, Natalie thought. Today is Monday, the first day of the week. Goody. Five days of school before the weekend.

Natalie liked school very much. She especially like Miss Colman. Miss Colman was her wonderful teacher at Stoneybrook Academy. Natalie was not so happy about the weekend. That was because there was

1

no school on the weekend. And when there was no school, Natalie sometimes felt lonely. She did not have many friends. And she did not have a single best friend. So on weekends hardly anyone ever came to her house to play. But during the week, Natalie saw the other kids at school.

Natalie switched on her light. She opened her wardrobe door. What did she feel like wearing to school that day? The other kids thought Natalie was a baby, so Natalie tried to find a grown-up-looking outfit. Her fuzzy kitten jumper? No. Her Barney and Baby Bop shirt? No way. Finally she settled on a plain red jumper and her blue jeans. Blue jeans were good because they would hide Natalie's socks, which were always falling down. Sometimes the kids at school teased Natalie about her drooping socks. Natalie did not know how the other kids managed to keep their own socks up. But she had decided not to spend much time worrying about it. Life was too short.

Natalie looked at the red jumper. She had

not worn it in a long time. She hoped it still fitted. She hoped—

"Hey!" Natalie cried. "What is *that*?" She was looking at something sewn inside the collar of her jumper. It was a small white tag. It read:

> Natalie Springer
> 62 Elm Street
> Stoneybrook, CT 06800

"Yuck!" Natalie shrieked. Where had *that* come from? What a horrible babyish tag. Natalie could not wear a jumper with a name tag in it. Name tags were for four-year-olds. Natalie was seven. She stuffed the jumper back on the shelf in the wardrobe. She pulled out a stripey jumper. She checked the collar. Another name tag! This was awful. Natalie looked in her kitten jumper. She looked in the Barney shirt. She looked in her jeans. Name tag, name tag, name tag.

Mrs Springer had gone on a sewing spree.

3

Everywhere Natalie looked she found another name tag. They were sewn in her underwear and her socks, in her dresses and shirts. Natalie found one on her pillowcase and two more on her sheets. She even found one sewn inside the knitted cap on Buzzy Bear, her beloved teddy.

"Mummy!" cried Natalie.

"What is it?" Mrs Springer hurried into Natalie's room. She was still wearing her nightgown. "Are you sick?"

"No! Mummy, why are these name tags everywhere?"

Mrs Springer smiled. "Oh. In case you get your clothes mixed up at ballet class or during gym or at a sleepover. We will always know which ones are yours."

Natalie sighed. She knew her mother was trying to help her. But this was no help at all.

2

UNDERWEAR

Natalie stood alone in her room. Her bed was covered with clothes. In every single one was a name tag. Natalie thought about cutting the tags off, but they were sewn in quite tightly. Besides, her mother had worked very hard. The sewing had taken her a long time.

Natalie reached for the red jumper and the jeans. And underwear and socks. Only her shoes had escaped name tags. She hoped the kids at school would not see the babyish tags, but she had a feeling they would be noticed one day. Probably very soon. And then the kids would chant, "Baby, baby, baby! Natalie's a baby!"

Well, that was not quite true, thought Natalie as she walked into her classroom that morning. Not all the kids would do that.

Natalie sat at her desk. She looked around. Natalie sat in the front row. That was because she wore glasses. Miss Colman thought the glasses-wearers could see better in the front row. Miss Colman knew about things like that. Miss Colman wore glasses herself. (And anyway, Miss Colman knew about lots of things.)

Natalie looked at Karen Brewer in the back row. Karen was one of the kids who probably would not tease Natalie. Karen was not a teaser. She talked too much, and she bragged and boasted and showed off. But she did not tease. (Usually.) Karen was lucky. She had *two* best friends, Hannie Papadakis and Nancy Dawes. Karen and Hannie and Nancy sat together in the last row. Hannie and Nancy probably would not tease Natalie, either.

Natalie watched as the other kids entered

the classroom. There were Ricky Torres, Bobby Gianelli and Hank Reubens. Definite teasers. There were Jannie Gilbert and Leslie Morris, best friends and more teasers. There were Tammy and Terri Barkan, the twins. They would not tease. They were Natalie's friends. There were Ian Johnson and Chris Lamar. Probably teasers, but it was hard to tell. There was Sara Ford. She was new that year, and would not tease. And there was Audrey Green, another definite teaser.

Natalie checked her clothes. Good. None of the tags showed. If she were very, *very*, VERY careful, perhaps she could keep them hidden.

When Miss Colman entered the room, Natalie began to feel more cheerful. First of all, Miss Colman always made her feel cheerful. Second, Natalie realized she had been sitting in her classroom for almost twenty minutes and no one had seen a name tag. That was a good sign. A very good sign.

Miss Colman picked up her book of lesson plans.

Knock knock.

Who was at the door? It was very early in the morning for a visitor.

Miss Colman opened the door to Room 2A. "Well! Hello, Mrs Springer," Natalie heard Miss Colman say.

Mrs Springer? What was Natalie's mother doing at the school?

Miss Colman and Mrs Springer stepped into the room. "Hi, Miss Colman," Mrs Springer replied. "I just brought this in for Natalie." Mrs Springer held up a brown paper bag. "She forgot it this morning. It is her underwear. Her ballet lesson is this afternoon, and Natalie needs a change of clothes." Mrs Springer waved to Natalie. Then she left.

Miss Colman gave the bag to Natalie. She sat down at her desk and looked at her lesson plans. Then she poked her head into Mr Berger's room next door. Mr Berger was the other second-grade teacher. A door joined the two classrooms.

Bobby grabbed the paper bag.

"I want to see Natalie's underwear!" he cried.

"Me, too!" shouted Hank.

Before Natalie knew it, every kid in her class had seen her underwear. And every kid had seen the name tags.

I am dead meat, said Natalie to herself.

OMAR

The moment Miss Colman returned to the classroom, the kids quietened down. Bobby tossed the underwear bag back to Natalie. Natalie stuffed it inside her desk. (She gave it a little pinch because she was cross with it.)

All around her, the kids were smirking. Bobby and Hank were turning red from trying not to laugh.

Miss Colman took the register. Natalie counted as Miss Colman made the ticks in her book. Tick, tick, tick ... fifteen ticks in all. Hmm. Someone was missing. Someone was absent.

"Girls and boys," said Miss Colman then.

"I have something to tell you. Omar is absent today. He is in the hospital."

"The *hos*pital?" exclaimed Karen Brewer.

"Yes," replied Miss Colman. "Omar cut his hand and the cut became infected. He will be in the hospital for just two days. And he will be back in school on Thursday. But I thought we might make Get Well cards for him. I can take them to the hospital this afternoon."

Natalie looked around the classroom. The kids had stopped giggling. They were not even smiling. They were all thinking about Omar and the hospital. This was serious.

Later that morning, Miss Colman handed out coloured paper and pens. Natalie carefully made a beautiful card for Omar. So did the other kids. They still looked very serious. Maybe they had forgotten about Natalie's underwear and the name tags.

On Thursday, Omar returned to school, just as Miss Colman had said he would. (That was one reason Natalie loved Miss Colman. Miss Colman always kept her

promises.) Omar's hand was in a bandage.
Otherwise, he seemed fine.

"Tell us about the hospital, Omar!"
begged Natalie's classmates.

"Omar can do that during Show and
Share," said Miss Colman.

When it was time for Show and Share,
Miss Colman called on Omar first.

"The hospital," Omar began, as he stood
before the class, "was very boring. The food
was not so great. But it was not bad, either.

The doctors and nurses were nice. I had lots of visitors. And I got some nice presents. But mostly I was bored, bored, bored."

Hmmm. Bored, thought Natalie. Now isn't that interesting.

4
NATALIE'S GREAT IDEA

After Omar sat down, Miss Colman took her place in the front of the classroom. "Now *I* have something to share with you," she said. "We are about to begin a new project. We will work on it together. As a class."

Natalie squirmed in her seat. She smiled to herself. This sounded exciting.

"It is a project," Miss Colman continued, "that another teacher thought up. She tried it with her second-grade class. I read about in a magazine.

"The project began," Miss Colman went

on, "when the teacher brought a teddy bear to school. The bear's name was Rudy. The teacher made a tag for Rudy and fastened it to his shirt. This is what the tag said: *My name is Rudy. I am on an adventure. When you find me, please take me with you for several days. Then leave me in a public place for someone else to find. Send a postcard about your adventure with me to this address.* And the teacher had written out the address of her classroom. She left Rudy in an airport. Sure enough, someone found Rudy. It was a woman on holiday. She wrote to the class saying she had taken Rudy to Florida. Rudy had gone to the beach with her, and then ridden on Space Mountain at Disney World. Then she left Rudy in a restaurant in the Magic Kingdom. And another person found Rudy. That person took Rudy to New York City. Very soon, the kids in the class were receiving postcards and letters and even photos of Rudy from all around the world. Rudy had lots of adventures."

"Cool!" exclaimed Hannie Papadakis.

"Awesome," said Chris Lamar.

Audrey Green raised her hand. "Did Rudy come back to the class?" she asked.

Miss Colman smiled. "Oh, yes. I forgot about that part. On the back of the tag, the teacher wrote: *If you find me after the fifteenth of March, please return me to the address on the front of this tag.* And sure enough, on the third of April, Rudy returned to school. Someone found him in Switzerland, and posted him back home."

"Excellent," said Ricky, nodding his head.

"And so," continued Miss Colman, "we are going to send a teddy bear on an adventure, too. We can follow its journey on a map, and learn about the places it visits."

"Does it have to be a teddy bear?" asked Jannie Gilbert.

"No," replied Miss Colman. "It could be a doll or another kind of stuffed animal."

"Where will we get the doll or stuffed animal?" asked Nancy Dawes.

"Anyone who wants to," said Miss

Colman, "may bring in a teddy or doll tomorrow. We will vote on which one will take the trip. And we will ask that it be sent back to us by the first of December."

Natalie was trying to pay attention to Miss Colman. But her mind was wandering. Just a little bit. It had wandered back to what Omar had said about the hospital. That the hospital was boring, boring, boring.

Natalie raised her hand. "Miss Colman?" she said. "I have an idea."

"Yes, Natalie?"

"I was thinking that when our project is over, we could put all the postcards and things in an album. Then we could take the album to the hospital. We could leave it there so the kids who are stuck in the hospital could read about the exciting adventure. Then they would not be so bored."

"Hey! That is a great idea!" cried Karen.

"Indoor voice, Karen," Miss Colman reminded her.

"It *is* a great idea," said Sara quietly.

Natalie looked around her. The other kids agreed. Natalie's idea was great.

"That is just what the kids in the hospital need," said Omar.

"We can make the album really special," said Leslie Morris.

Everyone began talking at once.

No one mentioned underwear. Or name tags.

Natalie smiled. Then she grinned.

She grinned at Miss Colman, and Miss Colman grinned back at her.

5

BUZZY BEAR

Natalie swallowed the last of her apple juice. She ate the last bite of her chocolate chip cookie. Then she carried the carton her juice had come in to a bin at the back of the cafeteria. It was a recycling bin, and Natalie was careful to recycle. It was important to her.

"Want to play hopscotch?" Terri Barkan asked when Natalie returned to the table. "Tammy and I are going to play."

"Yes please," replied Natalie. The kids had been really nice to her all morning. Natalie thought it was because of her good idea about giving the special project to the kids in the hospital.

On the playground, Terri and Tammy and Natalie found smooth stones for their hopscotch game. The twins let Natalie go first. As Natalie hopped along, Terri said to Tammy, "We could bring in Tootsie tomorrow."

"Tootsie? Who's Tootsie?" asked Natalie.

"Our stuffed elephant," replied Terri. "Maybe Tootsie could go on the adventure."

"Wait, you bring Tootsie, and I will bring

Taffy," said Tammy. "Taffy is our stuffed chipmunk," she told Natalie.

Sara Ford wandered by. She had stopped to watch the game. While Tammy took her turn, Sara said, "I am going to bring in my Barbie tomorrow."

"Your *Barbie*?" repeated Terri. "That is very brave. She might not come back, you know. Miss Colman said so."

"I know," replied Sara. "I will take that chance."

"Wow..." said Natalie slowly. That *was* brave of Sara. Miss Colman had indeed said there was a chance the teddy or doll that was sent on the trip might not be returned. It might get lost somewhere, or someone might decide to keep it (even though that would be stealing, Natalie noted). Or someone might decide that posting a teddy back to Stoneybrook, Connecticut, was just too much trouble.

"*I* am going to bring in Goosie tomorrow," said Karen Brewer. She was watching the game with Hannie and Nancy.

"You *are*? Your stuffed cat?" cried Hannie. "But you love Goosie."

"Well, I am brave, too," said Karen.

"And – and so am I," said Jannie Gilbert. "I am going to bring in Sleepytime Susie. My best doll."

"I wonder if the boys will be brave enough to bring in anything," said Karen. She glanced at Bobby and Omar playing football nearby.

"I heard that," said Omar. "And I am going to bring in my old giraffe."

24

"What are you going to bring, Natalie?" asked Nancy Dawes.

"I – I am going to bring . . . well, I have so many choices. I have not decided yet. I will decide tonight."

That night, Natalie sat on her bed. Spread out around her were her dolls and Buzzy Bear. Buzzy Bear was Natalie's only stuffed toy. She liked dolls better than teddies. Except for Buzzy Bear. Buzzy was Natalie's favourite toy in the world. He had been given to her by her grandfather on the day she was born. Natalie had never, ever spent a night without Buzzy. He came with her on holidays. He came with her on sleepovers. Could Natalie really part with Buzzy for two or three months? What if Buzzy never came back?

Natalie thought and thought. She wanted to be brave like the other kids. She wanted to show them she was not a baby, even if her mother *had* sewn name tags everywhere. Natalie looked at her dolls. She could bring in one of them. Maybe. Well, no. Her dolls were all quite tatty, and most of them were naked. The boys would tease her for ever if she brought in one of her dolls.

That left Buzzy Bear.

Natalie sighed. She laid Buzzy on her pillow.

"OK," she said to him. "Tomorrow you are going to have a special treat. Tomorrow I am going to take you to school with me."

6
TO WHOM IT MAY CONCERN

The next day, Buzzy Bear rode to school in Natalie's lap. Natalie was feeling a lot better than she had felt the night before. This was because she had thought of something wonderful. Natalie had realized that just because she brought Buzzy to school did not mean that Buzzy would go on the trip. Someone else's teddy would probably be chosen, and that would be just fine. Natalie could bring Buzzy to her room, and the kids would see how brave she was. But then they would choose a different toy, and Natalie could take Buzzy home with her at the end of the day. Perfect.

So now Natalie hopped out of the car. "'Bye, Daddy!" she called to her father. And she ran into school with Buzzy. She was not worried one little bit. "I hope you like school, Buzzy," she whispered.

Natalie sat at her desk. She put Buzzy in her lap. She watched the other kids arrive. Natalie decided she would try to guess which doll or animal would be chosen to make the trip. (She had a feeling it might be Sleepytime Susie.)

OK. There was Jannie. But where was Sleepytime Susie? Hmm. Jannie must have forgotten her.

And now there was Sara. But where was her Barbie?

Natalie saw Terri and Tammy, but no Tootsie or Taffy. She saw Karen, but no Goosie. And she saw Omar, but no old giraffe.

Soon all of Natalie's classmates had arrived. And their desks were empty except for Buzzy Bear. Natalie could not stand it.

She turned around and whispered to Tammy, "Where is Taffy?"

"I, um, decided not to bring her," replied Tammy.

"You mean, you chickened out," said Hank.

"Well, you were going to bring in your firefighter doll," said Tammy. "And I do not see that anywhere."

"I for*got* it!" cried Hank.

"Liar," said Ian. "You chickened out, too. So did Omar."

"So did everyone," muttered Natalie.

Natalie looked at Buzzy. He was sitting on her desk wearing his knitted hat and coat. Natalie thought about stuffing him inside the desk, but he was too big for that. Besides, all the kids had seen him.

Later that morning, Miss Colman stood before her class. "Where are your dolls and soft toys?" she asked.

The kids pointed silently to Buzzy Bear.

"That's it?" said Miss Colman. "No one brought in anything else?"

The kids shook their heads.

"Well, then. Hmm." Miss Colman smiled at Natalie. "It looks like we do not even need to take a vote. Buzzy Bear it is. I hope you are ready for a big adventure, Buzzy."

Natalie tried to smile back at Miss Colman.

Just then, Bobby Gianelli, of all people, tapped Natalie's arm. "You are really brave," he said to her.

"*Really* brave," added Audrey from behind her.

Natalie gulped. She nodded. She could not back out. Not now when the kids finally thought she was grown-up, and even brave.

Miss Colman picked Buzzy up. "Well, let's see," she said. "I like your blue and yellow coat very much. It is the perfect thing to pin your travelling note to. Class, we are going to write Buzzy's note together. I will write it on the blackboard for now. When it is finished, we can copy it on to a tag for Buzzy. OK. How should we begin our letter?"

31

Omar waved his hand in the air. "I know!
It should start: To whom it may concern."
On the blackboard, Miss Colman printed:

To Whom It May Concern:

7
GOODBYE, BUZZY BEAR

To Whom It May Concern:

Hello! My name is Buzzy Bear. I belong to Class 2A at Stoneybrook Academy in Stoneybrook, Connecticut. I would like to have some adventures. The kids in 2A would like to learn about other cities and countries. Please take me with you for a day or two. Then send a postcard or a letter or a photo to the address on the back of this tag so the kids in 2A will know what I have been up to. When our adventure is over, leave me in a place where someone else can find me. Eventually, Class 2A would like to have me back so I can go home with Natalie Springer, who is my owner. Please return me by 1st December. Thank you!

That was the message Miss Colman had written on a big cardboard tag. On the back of the tag, she had printed the address of Stoneybrook Academy. Then she had fastened the tag to Buzzy Bear's coat with a large safety pin.

"There," said Miss Colman when she had finished.

Now Buzzy Bear was sitting on the edge of her desk. It was a very important day. Today Buzzy would leave on his adventure. When the kids in Miss Colman's class entered their room that morning, Buzzy was the first thing they saw.

"Hi, Buzzy Bear," said Natalie as she sat at her desk. "Are you ready to go on your trip? You will be leaving soon."

"Are *you* ready to let Buzzy go on his trip?" Miss Colman asked Natalie.

Natalie nodded. "Yes." She was not going to let her classmates down.

Shortly before lunchtime, Natalie heard a knock at the door. She looked up from her reading book. Miss Colman was opening the door.

"Hello, Susan," she said.

"Hello." A smiling woman entered the room. She was carrying a briefcase. She looked at Miss Colman's desk. "Is that Buzzy Bear?"

"It certainly is," replied Miss Colman. Miss Colman faced her class. "Girls and boys," she said, "this is my friend Susan Ying. She is going on a business trip today. She has agreed to take Buzzy Bear with her to the airport. She will leave him for the first person to find."

"Are you ready for your trip, Buzzy?" asked Susan Ying.

Buzzy just sat on Miss Colman's desk. The tag was so big that it hid part of his face. Natalie could see only one of his eyes.

Natalie raised her hand. "Um, Miss Ying?" she said. "I am Natalie Springer. Buzzy is my bear. And I think he is ready for the trip. Do you know where

you will leave him when you get to the airport?"

"I think I will leave him in a waiting area – at a gate where a lot of people are waiting for a flight. Either that or I will leave him in a restaurant at the airport."

Natalie nodded. "OK."

Miss Colman handed Buzzy to Susan Ying. "Thank you so much for doing this," she said. "We really appreciate it."

"I am happy to do it," replied Miss Ying. "I will call you later."

"Goodbye! Goodbye, Buzzy!" called the kids as Miss Ying carried him out of the door. "Have a good trip!"

"Goodbye, Buzzy!" Natalie called along with her friends. Then she whispered, "I love you."

Just before the bell rang at the end of the day, the office secretary came to the door of 2A. He handed a slip of paper to Miss Colman. Miss Colman read it. Then she turned to her pupils. "Class," she said, "this message is from Susan Ying. She phoned to say that she left Buzzy in a crowd of people waiting for a plane to Chicago.''

Chicago, thought Natalie. That sounded awfully far away.

8

HELLO FROM CHICAGO

When the kids in Miss Colman's class entered their room the next day, they saw something new. Miss Colman had taken down the leaf pictures that had been tacked to the noticeboard. In their place was an enormous map. It was a map of every country in the world.

"That," said Miss Colman, "is to help us keep track of Buzzy's trip. Each time we get a postcard from Buzzy, we will see where the card is from. We will circle that place on the map. And we will draw a line from there to the next place Buzzy visits. While

we wait to hear from Buzzy, we can learn about the places he visits."

Natalie felt very impatient that morning. She had trouble sitting still. She wriggled and squirmed.

Finally she raised her hand. "Miss Colman? When does the postman come to our school?"

"You mean what time of day? Lunchtime, I think," said Miss Colman.

After break that day, Natalie hurried to

her seat. "Miss Colman, Miss Colman! Is the post here yet? Did we get a postcard from Buzzy?"

"Oh, Natalie. It is too soon to hear from Buzzy," said Miss Colman. "I am sorry. I do not think we will hear from him for several more days."

"Several more *days*? Boo." Natalie slumped in her seat. How could she wait for several more days?

She did wait, of course. And on Tuesday

afternoon when the kids in Miss Colman's class returned to their seats after lunch, their teacher was smiling. "I have great news," she said. She was holding a postcard.

"You heard from Buzzy!" shrieked Natalie. "What does the card say?"

Miss Colman held it up so her students could see the picture. "It is a photo of the city of Chicago," said Miss Colman. "And this is what Buzzy wrote: 'Dear Class Two-A, hello from the great city of Chicago! Right now I am travelling with Mr Frank Saunders. He found me at the airport and took me on a plane with him. So far I have been to the Sears Tower, eaten lunch at the Hard Rock Cafe and gone to a very boring business meeting. Yours truly, Buzzy.'"

Natalie heaved a deep sigh. Buzzy was safe. And he was having fun (except for the boring meeting). She raised her hand. "What is the Sears Tower?" she asked. "I want to learn about Chicago!"

9

Buzzy in London

During the next few days, the kids in Miss Colman's class were very busy. Miss Colman helped them find Chicago, Illinois, on the big map. Omar circled it with a red marker pen.

"I wonder where Buzzy will go next," said Audrey.

While they waited to find out, they learned about Chicago and about Illinois. They learned that the state bird of Illinois is the cardinal, and the state flower is the violet.

"Let's find out the bird and the flower for every state," said Karen. So they started a list.

They learned that Chicago is the largest city in Illinois, but that it is not the capital. The capital is Springfield. They learned that Illinois is sometimes called the Prairie State. Then they looked up some information about the Sears Tower. They found out that it is a skyscraper 110 storeys high.

On Friday, another postcard arrived. This one said:

Dear Class 2A,

Hi, it is me, your friend Buzzy Bear! I am in Dallas, Texas, now. A girl found me in the airport in Chicago. (She is writing this for me.) Her name is Nora, and she is eleven. Nora took me to a Dallas Cowboys football game with her dad. The Cowboys won! It was really exciting!

Love,
Buzzy

Four days later a letter arrived. It was from Wyoming. A man and a woman and their new baby had found Buzzy in a restaurant in Dallas. They took Buzzy with them on their holiday.

Chris Lamar had opened the letter. He was reading it to the class. "Hey! Here is a photo of Buzzy! He is riding a horse near . . . near . . . Grand Teton National Park." Chris held up the photo of Buzzy on horseback.

The kids in Miss Colman's class circled two more cities on the map. They learned about Texas and Wyoming.

One day a card arrived with a different looking stamp.

"The card is from Canada!" exclaimed Bobby. "Buzzy is in another country. He is a foreign traveller."

A woman named Gina Seldon had found Buzzy in a department store. She had flown him to Calgary, Alberta.

"Brrrr! It is *cold* here," Buzzy wrote.

After the card from Alberta arrived, the kids did not hear from Buzzy for one whole long week. Finally, one Wednesday afternoon, Miss Colman was holding up a letter

when her class returned from lunch. She was smiling again. In fact, she was grinning. "You will never guess where this letter is from," she said.

"Is it from Alaska?" suggested Jannie.

"No. That is a good guess, though," said Miss Colman. "Hank, why don't you read the letter to us."

Hank walked to the front of the room. He unfolded the thin sheet of blue paper. "'Dear Class Two-A,'" he read. "'Hello! It is me, Buzzy Bear. I am in London, England. Emily and Kathryn Shulman and their mum have taken me to the Tower of London and two museums. . .'"

The letter went on and on.

London, England, thought Natalie. What an adventure Buzzy is having. He is so lucky.

Buzzy's next card was from Paris, France. The next was from Milan, Italy and the next was from Warsaw in Poland.

"He is a world traveller," Natalie announced proudly to her classmates. And they agreed, wide-eyed. "I wonder where he will go next," added Natalie.

She waited to hear. Her classmates waited to hear. Miss Colman waited to hear. But two entire weeks crawled by with no word at all.

10

WHERE IS BUZZY?

At the end of two weeks, Natalie was worried. Buzzy was so far away. He had taken such a long trip. Until now, this had seemed wonderful. The classroom map was full of red circles. It was criss-crossed with red lines. The list of state birds and flowers was growing. And the kids had decided to make another list: state nicknames. Their state, Connecticut, was known as the Nutmeg State, which they thought was funny.

But now Natalie could not help worrying about Buzzy. Two weeks was a very long time. Where could he be? What could have happened?

"Well," said Miss Colman, "remember

that Buzzy is in Europe now. Lots and lots of different languages are spoken there. Maybe Buzzy has been found by someone who does not speak English. He would not be able to read Buzzy's tag. And he could not write a card or a letter for Buzzy."

Natalie tried to feel hopeful. But it was hard. Even Miss Colman did not look very hopeful. She frowned each time the post came, and there was no word from Buzzy.

After two more weeks went by, Natalie began to feel frightened. Now Buzzy had not been heard from in a month. She had known all along that it was possible – just possible – that Buzzy might be left somewhere and not found. Or that someone might find him who would not care about the class project. Someone could give Buzzy away, or put him somewhere and forget about him.

But *maybe*, Natalie said to herself, Miss Colman is right. Someone, or several some-ones, have found Buzzy, but cannot read his tag. I will just have to keep waiting and hoping.

One evening, Natalie sat at the dinner table with her parents. She was trying to eat, but she was not very hungry.

"Is anything wrong?" asked Mr Springer.

"We have not heard from Buzzy in a month," replied Natalie.

"That is a long time," said her mother.

"Yes." Natalie swallowed hard.

"We know you miss him," said her father.

"Yes," said Natalie again.

"And maybe you will hear from him soon," added Mr Springer. "A letter could come any day. Perhaps tomorrow."

Natalie nodded. Her parents wanted her to feel better. But when Natalie went to bed that night, she began to cry. She lay on her back and let the tears run down the sides of her face and into her ears.

She sniffled loudly. "Where are you, Buzzy Bear?" she asked. "I miss you." Natalie pulled aside her curtain. She stared outside at the full round moon. "Do you know, Man-in-the-moon?"

The man in the moon did not answer. After a long time, Natalie fell asleep.

That night, she did not sleep very well. She dreamed about Buzzy Bear. She dreamed that he was lost in a supermarket. He ran up and down the aisles, looking for Natalie. He tried to ask for help, but it turned out to be a French supermarket, and Buzzy did not speak French.

The next day, Natalie felt grumpy. She ate her breakfast silently. She rode to school with her father silently.

"Goodbye, Natalie! Have a good day at school!" called Mr Springer.

"'Bye," was all Natalie replied.

That morning Miss Colman collected homework and took the register. Then she stood in front of her class. She looked very serious.

Uh-oh, thought Natalie.

"Boys and girls, I would like to talk to you about something," Miss Colman began. "It is about Buzzy. We have not heard about him in over a month now, which is a long time. I am afraid I must tell you that I think there is a good chance Buzzy will not be coming back."

A SURPRISE
FOR NATALIE

Natalie stared at Miss Colman.

"I am sorry, Natalie," said her teacher.

Natalie nodded. Her stomach hurt, as if someone had just kicked it. Natalie thought, I knew all along that Buzzy might not come back. But . . . I never believed it would happen.

Now that Natalie had heard Miss Colman say so, though, it suddenly seemed very very real.

"Natalie?" asked Miss Colman.

Natalie could not speak. Before she knew what was happening, she began to cry.

Tears slid down her cheeks. She wiped them away, but she could not stop crying. All the other kids were looking at her.

And then Bobby began to snigger. So did Leslie. So did Jannie and Ian and Audrey. Hee, hee, hee. Their hands covered their mouths, but Natalie could hear them anyway. She could hear them just fine.

Natalie wiped away a few more tears in time to stare at the laughers. She gave them a Very Stern Look. With a Very Big Frown. She looked quite cross.

The gigglers stopped giggling.

"All right," said Miss Colman. "That is enough. Calm down, please. It is time for our science work, anyway. But first, let me see. I believe Mr Posner left some papers in the office for me. Natalie, would you please go and get them?"

Natalie stood up. She stalked out of the room.

As soon as she was gone, Miss Colman said to her class, "Can you tell me why you laughed at Natalie just now?" She

56

looked at Bobby, Jannie, Leslie, Ian and Audrey.

No one said a word.

"I am serious," Miss Colman went on. "I would really like to know why you laughed at her."

Bobby, Jannie, Leslie, Ian and Audrey were staring down at their desks. Finally, Ian looked up. He raised his hand. "Um, because she was crying," he mumbled.

"And you thought that was funny?" Miss Colman said.

"Well, it is just that sometimes Natalie is such a baby."

"Why do you think she was crying?" asked Miss Colman. "Jannie?"

"Because she feels sad."

At the back of the room, Karen Brewer was wriggling around in her seat. She was waving her hand. "Miss Colman! Miss Colman!"

"Yes, Karen?"

"Miss Colman, Natalie was crying because she feels bad that Buzzy Bear is not coming back. Buzzy is Natalie's only bear. She loves him very much. But still, she brought him to school and she let him go on the trip. That was very brave of her." Karen paused. "Nobody *else* let any of *their* toys go," she said sternly.

"Thank you, Karen," said Miss Colman.

Bobby raised his hand. "Maybe," he said slowly, "maybe we should do something nice for Natalie. Something to make her feel better."

"That would be a lot better than laughing at her," said Karen huffily.

"OK, Karen. That is enough," said Miss Colman.

Audrey brightened then. "I know! We could get another bear for Natalie. We could even get her another Buzzy Bear, exactly like the one she lost. I have seen them in Bellair's, the department store."

"Now *that* is a great idea," said Miss Colman.

"We could all chip in some money," added Sara.

"And we could *surprise* Natalie with her new Buzzy," said Nancy.

"Fantastic," agreed Miss Colman. "And now, class, Natalie will be back at any moment. So please open your books. And zip up your lips."

BUZZY TWO

Natalie hurried along the corridor. She was carrying an envelope for Miss Colman from Mr Posner. It looked important. And Natalie felt important to have been trusted with it. She opened the door to 2A. Her classmates were reading their science books. They seemed very, very interested in them. Natalie handed the envelope to her teacher. "Thank you, Natalie," said Miss Colman.

"You're welcome."

Natalie returned to her seat. She was glad that no one said anything else to her. She was especially glad that no one giggled.

That afternoon, Natalie realized something very interesting. It was about Buzzy Bear. Natalie realized that she was doing all right without him. She still loved Buzzy, of course. And she missed him, and was very sad that he was gone. But she was doing all right. After all, Buzzy had now been away for quite a while. And Natalie was still much the same. Or better. She had brought home an extra good report. She had played at Karen's house a couple of times. She had even lost two teeth and grown another centimetre. Her mother thought her feet were growing again, too, and that soon Natalie would need new shoes.

All this without Buzzy, thought Natalie. Mm.

On Monday morning, Natalie hurried into the classroom. The bell was about to ring. The rest of the kids were already sitting at their desks. They grinned at Natalie as she ran to her seat.

Uh-oh, thought Natalie. I wonder what is wrong. She checked her clothes. No name

tags were sticking out. Her underwear was not showing. She pulled up her socks. No one said anything. But no one stopped smiling, either.

After the morning announcements, Miss Colman said, "Jannie? Karen? Would you come to the front of the room, please?"

Grinning more widely than ever, Jannie and Karen flew to the front of the room. They pulled a box out from under Miss

Colman's desk. Together they picked it up and set it on Natalie's desk.

"Natalie, this is for you from all of us," said Jannie.

"To say thank you for letting Buzzy go on the trip," added Karen.

"Oh—" Natalie started to say.

But Karen hurried on. "It was really, really nice of you to lend us Buzzy," she said. "No one else was brave enough to let their bears go away. We really, really appreciate what you did. And we—"

"And we want to say thank you," said Miss Colman quickly.

"You're welcome," said Natalie.

"Open your present!" cried Karen.

Natalie looked at the big box. She untied the ribbon. She tore off the wrapping paper. Then she lifted the lid of the box, and pulled away some tissue paper. Staring up at her were the black button eyes of Buzzy Bear. Not her own Buzzy, Natalie realized. But another bear that looked very much like Buzzy. He was even wearing Buzzy's knitted hat and his blue and yellow coat.

"Wow," said Natalie. "Um, thanks. Thanks a lot."

"Guess what his name is," said Karen. "It is Buzzy Two."

"Buzzy Two," repeated Natalie. "Well . . . well, thanks."

When Natalie returned home from school that day, she took Buzzy Two to her room. She sat him on her bed in Buzzy's old spot. But he did not look quite right there. So Natalie moved him to her bookshelf. She put him with some other toys.

Natalie knew a secret. Her secret was that she liked Buzzy Two. But she did not need him.

LOVE, MARY

Another week went by without a word from Buzzy. It was almost winter now. The days were short and cold.

One afternoon when Natalie's mother picked her up after school, she said, "Darling, a package came for you today."

"What?" said Natalie. She had not been listening. She had been looking out of the car window at the dark sky. She was wondering if it might snow soon. "I got a package?" she said.

"Yes. All the way from Ireland. Isn't that odd? We do not know anyone in Ireland."

"Ireland," repeated Natalie. "I know where that is." She thought of the map on the wall in her classroom. "It is near Scotland. The capital is Dublin. Who is the package from?"

"Someone named Mary Bowen."

Hmmm. Mary Bowen. Natalie wondered about Mary and the package all the way home. As soon as her mother parked the car, Natalie hopped out. She ran inside. The package was lying on a table in the hallway.

"Here, Natalie. Let me help you," said Mrs Springer. She found a pair of scissors and cut the tape that was wound around the box.

Natalie looked at the address. Just as her mother had said, the box had been posted by Mary Bowen from Dublin, Ireland.

"Her handwriting looks just like mine, Mummy," said Natalie. "I bet Mary Bowen is seven, too."

"But who on earth could she be?" asked Mrs Springer.

When the tape had been cut away, Natalie opened up the box. The first thing she saw was an envelope with her name on it. Natalie opened the envelope. She pulled out a letter. It said:

Dear Natalie,

You do not know me. My name is Mary Bowen. I am eight years old. I live in Dublin, Ireland. That is very far away from you. I suppose you are wondering how I got your name and address. Well, that is a good story. I found them inside the hat of this bear.

"This bear!" cried Natalie. "This *bear*?!"

Natalie let Mary's letter fall to the floor. She shoved aside the newspaper in the box. And she pulled out ... Buzzy Bear.

"The *real* Buzzy!" Natalie cried. "Oh, he is *back*! Mary found Buzzy and she sent him *back*! But why didn't she send him to school? That was what the note on his tag said to do. And *where* did she find my address? Oh, my goodness. I cannot believe Buzzy is back!"

Mrs Springer was smiling. "Buzzy's tag must have come off," she said. "See, Natalie?

FROM: MARY BOWEN,
DUBLIN,
IRELAND

He looks a little bedraggled. Now let's see how Mary found your home address." Mrs Springer took off Buzzy's cap.

"Oh! Oh, it is the name tag!" exclaimed Natalie. "You sewed one of my name tags in Buzzy's hat! Gosh, I thought that was silly when you did it. But now I am glad!"

Natalie read the rest of Mary's letter. It told how Mary had found Buzzy while she was waiting in the Dublin airport. He was stuck behind a seat. Mary had started to play with Buzzy when she saw the name tag with Natalie's address on it. The end of her letter said:

I knew you would want your teddy back. If he were mine and I lost him, I would want him back. So I am sending him to you now. My mum is helping me. (She is the person my dad and I were waiting to meet at the airport.) Have fun with your bear.

Love,
Mary

"Oh, this is too wonderful!" said Natalie.

"This was awfully nice of Mary," added Mrs Springer.

"I want to write to her and thank her. Can I?" asked Natalie.

"Of course."

So Natalie settled down at the kitchen table. A piece of her mother's best writing paper was in front of her. In her lap sat Buzzy.

Dear Mary, Natalie began.

NATALIE'S GIFT

That night, Natalie slept with Buzzy Bear again. It was just like old times. Except that when Natalie woke the next morning, she found Buzzy on the floor. "You must have fallen out of bed during the night," she said. "And I did not even notice."

When Natalie left for school later, Buzzy was tucked under her arm. In her school bag was the letter from Mary.

"Hey, you brought Buzzy Two to school!" exclaimed Jannie, when Natalie entered the classroom. "That's nice."

Natalie just smiled. She did not say anything.

Not until Show and Share.

But during Show and Share time, Natalie brought her bear to the front of the class. Then she read Mary's letter aloud.

"You mean that is the *real* Buzzy Bear?" cried Jannie.

"Oh, Natalie. How wonderful," said Miss Colman.

The kids gathered around Buzzy. They examined him. They looked at the name tag in his hat. (They did not laugh.)

"Well," said Miss Colman, "I suppose we will never know exactly what happened to Buzzy. We will never know how he got from Poland to Ireland, how he lost his tag, or how he got stuffed down behind a seat in the airport. But at least he is back."

"So we have an end to our story," said Chris.

"We could finish the book about his adventures," added Natalie.

"And take it to the hospital," said Omar.

The kids set to work. They got out all of the postcards, letters and photos from

Buzzy. They lined them up in the order they had received them. Then they found a small map of the world, one that would fit in an album. They traced Buzzy's journey on it. They copied their lists of state birds and flowers and nicknames.

Miss Colman let Natalie make the cover for the book about Buzzy. Natalie wrote THE ADVENTURES OF BUZZY BEAR in very beautiful letters. Under it, she glued a picture of Buzzy.

Then the kids began the job of gluing everything into the album. The first thing they glued down was the story of their project. Then they glued down the things Buzzy had sent from his trip. They wrote a caption under each one to explain what it was.

When Mary's letter had been glued down on the last page, Miss Colman said, "I think our project is ready."

Natalie raised her hand. "Almost ready," she said. "I have one more thing to go with the album." Natalie stood up. She walked to Miss Colman's desk. She set Buzzy Bear on the album.

"Oh, that is lovely, Natalie," said Miss Colman. "You are going to let the kids at the hospital see Buzzy in person."

"No," said Natalie. "I am going to *give* them Buzzy. I do not need him any more. But I bet the kids in the hospital do."

"Why don't you give them Buzzy Two?" asked Nancy.

Natalie shook her head. "You gave me Buzzy Two. He was a present from all of you. That was very special. So I do not want to give him away. But the kids in the hospital should have the real Buzzy to go with the album."

Miss Colman was smiling at Natalie. Natalie smiled back. Then she grinned at her classmates.

"Hey, I have an idea," said Audrey. "Miss Colman, could Mr Berger take a picture of us with Buzzy and the album? We could hang it on our noticeboard. Then we will always remember Buzzy and his trip and our project."

So Mr Berger came into the room with his Polaroid camera.

"Say cheese!" he said.

THE ADVENTURES OF BUZZY BEAR

"Is it time to line up?"

"Wait, I cannot find my boots."

"Is Buzzy Bear ready? Where is the album?"

"Karen, you are my partner today."

Natalie looked around the classroom. Everyone was very excited. In just a few minutes they would climb on a yellow school bus and ride to the hospital. It was time to visit the kids there, and give them Buzzy and the album.

"OK, class. Line up at the door," said Miss Colman.

The kids found their bus partners. They lined up with them by the door. Then they followed Miss Colman down the corridor, out of the front door and into the car park. Natalie's mother and the twins' father followed behind *them*. (They were the parent helpers for the trip.)

"All aboard!" called the bus driver.

Natalie and Hannie were the first two on the bus. Natalie carried Buzzy, and Hannie carried the album.

"Everybody! Everybody! I have to tell you something!" called Omar. He was waving his hand back and forth.

"Yes, what is it?" asked Miss Colman as the bus turned on to the street.

"I have to tell everyone about the hospital," said Omar. "Since I was in it not long ago, I know all about it. Now," he went on, "kids usually are *not* allowed to visit people in the hospital, not even other kids. So we will not be able to see the playroom in the kids' wing. The playroom is where the nurses will probably put Buzzy and the

78

album after we leave today. And it is very boring. There are just a few broken-down old toys in it, but Buzzy will cheer it up."

"Omar is right," said Miss Colman. "We cannot go upstairs when we get to the hospital. We are going to go to a special room downstairs. The doctors and nurses are going to bring some kids there to meet us. They are kids who do not have to worry about catching germs from us."

"They probably have broken legs and stuff," said Omar importantly. "They will be really glad to see us."

Natalie glanced at Hannie. "Are you nervous?" she asked.

"A little," said Hannie.

"Me, too," said Natalie. She clutched Buzzy Bear tightly.

A few minutes later, the bus pulled up in front of the hospital.

"Last stop!" called the driver.

Miss Colman led the kids inside.

A doctor met them at the door. "You must be the kids in Miss Colman's class,' she said. "My name is Dr Longwood. Thank you so much for coming. The children are waiting for you."

Dr Longwood took the kids to a big room. It was decorated with streamers and balloons. Natalie saw that eight kids were waiting for them. Many of them were in wheelchairs. Two kids were on crutches. One girl was bald.

At first, Natalie and her friends did not know what to say or do. So Miss Colman told the story of Buzzy and his adventures. Then she explained that her pupils were going to give the kids the album. "Along with something else," she added. "Natalie?"

"Along with the real Buzzy," said Natalie, and she held him up.

"Cool," said the girl who was bald.

"Is he really for us?" asked a boy in a wheelchair.

"He really is," replied Natalie. She handed Buzzy to the boy.

The kids crowded around. They patted

Buzzy. They looked at the name tag. They turned the pages in the album.

"Buzzy is famous!" exclaimed one girl.

"Thank you for Buzzy," another girl said to Natalie.

"You're welcome," replied Natalie.

The kids in Miss Colman's class visited for a while. When it was time to go, they called goodbye to Dr Longwood and the kids. Then they turned to leave. And Natalie whispered, "Goodbye, Buzzy. I still love you."

THE KIDS IN · MISS COLMAN'S CLASS

A new series by
Ann M. Martin

5.

THE SNOW WAR

After lunch Ian ran outside with *They Came from Beyond* and *Beyond Space* stuffed into a big pocket in his jacket. He ran straight to his tree, and he sat on the rock. He looked out over the playground. And he saw his classmates gathering at their forts again.

"Oh, no," said Ian with a groan.

"Get out of here! Get out of my way!" Ian heard Audrey yell.

"No, you *girls* get away from *our* fort!" Bobby yelled back.

"You do not own this playground!" cried Karen.

Terri threw the first snowball. Hank

threw the second. And Audrey threw the third. She threw it very hard. She was aiming at Ricky. But she missed. The snowball sailed across the playground. And it hit . . .

. . . Ian.

It hit him in the face.

YOUNG HIPPO FUNNY

Have a giggle with a Young Hippo Funny!

Bod's Mum's Knickers
Bod's Mum has some ENORMOUS
and very useful knickers!
Peter Beere

Metal Muncher
Life's not easy when your baby brother likes to ... *eat metal* !
Kathy Henderson

Count Draco Down Under
Stacey has a strange new visitor – he's a VAMPIRE!
Ann Jungman

Emily H and the Enormous Tarantula
Emily H and the Stranger in the Castle
Emily H Turns Detective
Three funny books about Emily H and her special pet –
Theo, the world's most enormous TARANTULA!
Kara May

Professor Blabbermouth on the Moon
Tonight's the night for Operation Moon Cheese!
Nigel Watts

The Pirate Band
Captain Tump and his Pirate Band sail the high seas
in search of new treasure...
Ann Ruffell

YOUNG HIPPO MAGIC

Anything is possible in these enchanting stories from
Young Hippo Magic!

My Friend's a Gris-Quok!
Alex has a deep, dark secret. He's half Gris-Quok!
Malorie Blackman

Diggory and the Boa Conductor
Why do MAGICAL things happen to ordinary Diggory?

The Little Pet Dragon
James's puppy is glimmering with magic!
Philippa Gregory

Broomstick Services
One day Joe, Lucy and Jackie find *three witches*!
Ann Jungman